Rooney

Captain
Forsythe

Worzel

The   Crowman

Mrs O'Riley

This edition published exclusively
for Marks and Spencer p.l.c.
by Purnell Books, Paulton, Bristol BS18 5LQ, a member of the
BPCC group of companies

ISBN 0 361 06006 8

The television series "Worzel Gummidge" starring Jon Pertwee
is devised and written by Keith Waterhouse and Willis Hall,
based upon the characters created by Barbara Euphan Todd.

St Michael

WORZEL GUMMIDGE
King of the Scarecrows

Adapted from the original television scripts by Susannah Bradley
Illustrated by Val Biro

Worzel Gummidge Goes to Ireland

Worzel Gummidge ran along the country lane after Aunt Sally, his progress hampered by the need to stop every two yards or so to pick up a flower which she tossed, disdainfully, over her shoulder.

"She loves me, she loves me not, she loves me not not . . . Aunt Sally, you's dropping all the pretty flowers I pinched for you!" he wailed.

Aunt Sally sniffed and tossed the rest of the bunch over her shoulder before mincing off, smirking.

Worzel sank into the hedgerow and sat there, blubbing, for some time. At last Aunt Sally returned.

"You revolting, common scarecrow, what do you think you are doing?" she roared.

"Weepin' an' snivellin', Aunt Sally," replied Worzel.

"And what are my pretty flowers doing lying about on the dirty, filthy ground?" demanded Aunt Sally.

"You chucked 'em there," said Worzel reasonably.

Aunt Sally looked haughtily at him.

"Dropped them, you mean. For a gentleman to pick up. So get on with it, you half-witted haybag!"

As Worzel placed the flowers in half a bottle of milk which he had about his person, Aunt Sally noticed a party of angry people approaching in a milk float.

"What nasty, common, vulgar human people," she said, taking the bottle from Worzel.

He looked.

"We'd best run for it," he said, panicking.

"*We?*" said Aunt Sally. "What is your predicament to me?"

"Because those are their flowers and milk bottle," said Worzel. Quick as a flash, they disappeared into the hedge.

Finding nothing but a scarecrow in a field, the local antique dealer, Miss Lewisham, her crony Miss Fosdyke and the milkman were about to leave the scene when their attention was caught by a flash of white material in the ditch.

"It's Mr. Shepherd's Aunt Sally," said Miss Lewisham in surprise. Not one to miss a bargain, she piled Aunt Sally onto the milk float.

"Don't 'ee worry your little wooden head, Aunt Sally," said Worzel softly. "Wherever they're taking you, old Worzel'll come and fetch 'ee back."

Miss Lewisham had no intention of taking Aunt Sally very far. As she explained a little later on the telephone to Mr. Shepherd, she had no intention of delivering it personally to him. In her shop it was, and there it would remain until he fetched it. Unless . . . Miss Lewisham noticed that a customer seemed very interested in the item. Perhaps Mr. Shepherd would care to sell it? Very well.

"I'll send you a cheque at once," said Miss Lewisham, and rang off. Then she went over to the customer and sold it to him for considerably more than she had agreed with Mr. Shepherd.

"How soon can you ship this across to me?" asked the customer. Miss Lewisham looked at the card he handed her.

On it were the words: *Professor Hagerty, Ballydoon Museum of Folk History*.

"Ireland? At once," said Miss Lewisham quickly, before he could change his mind.

Outside the door Worzel nodded and repeated the same word over and over to himself.

"Ireland. Ireland . . ."

Shuffling along the road he bumped into the Crowman.

"Ireland . . . ooer, Mr. Crowman, sir! Just shaking the rats out of my straw, not in that nice clean field, see. Where's Ireland, your honour? My Aunt Sally wants to know."

"Across the sea, Worzel. The Irish Sea. Why—is she emigrating, Worzel?"

"No, sir—it's just the way she walks, sir," said Worzel, and shuffled off.

When the Crowman was out of sight, Worzel stopped pretending to hobble towards Ten Acre Field and turned back towards Miss Lewisham's shop.

"And wherever this Irish Sea is, I'll find it, and I'll follow Aunt Sally. I'll follow and follow her until there's no followin' left!" he muttered to himself.

On the quayside at Dublin an unusual parcel was being hoisted ashore from one of the ships. It was mainly wrapped in brown paper, but the head and feet of Aunt Sally were visible to anyone who cared to look. One who could see nothing else was a certain scarecrow who was being frogmarched along to the Captain by a deckhand, on a charge of stowing away.

"Oi!" cried Worzel, as Aunt Sally was loaded on to a lorry. "Where are you taking that there parcel?"

"Ballydoon!" cried the driver of the lorry, starting up the engine.

"Ballydoon," repeated Worzel to himself. "Ballydoon. Ballydoon."

He was still chanting Ballydoon when, on the orders of the irate Captain, one of the deckhands threw him in the River Liffey. Still chanting it, he hauled himself out and made his way inland. Footsore and weary, and covered in seaweed, he trudged along.

Aunt Sally's journey was no more comfortable. The lorry bumped and jolted her so much that when the driver was forced to brake suddenly on meeting a herd of cows, Aunt Sally, brown paper and all, fell against the tailboard. Crash! went the tailboard, falling down, and out rolled Aunt Sally onto the road.

"Go away, you beast!" she snapped at a cow, who ambled over to lick her face. Struggling out of the brown paper, she tottered off.

Meanwhile, Worzel had reached a signpost, which he could not understand, not having brought his reading head with him. However, the sight of a labourer scything grass brought fresh hope.

"Oi!" yelled Worzel.

"Good day to you. And all you wish yourself," said the labourer, whose name was Rooney.

"Never mind all that," said Worzel tetchily. "Have you seen a brown paper parcel?"

"I have," said Rooney.

"Which way did it go?" asked Worzel.

"It went into the boot cupboard," replied Rooney without hesitation. "All except for the paper and string, and that was put away in the knife drawer."

"They stuffed my Aunt Sally in a boot cupboard?" roared Worzel.

"No, just the parcel, as far as I know. It had the boots in it, you see," said Rooney.

Worzel gave up in disgust and tramped off, along the road to Mulconny, not Ballydoon, although as he could not understand the signpost he had no idea of that.

"Another tinker, by the looks of him," said Mrs. O'Riley to her friend Mrs. O'Rourke, keeper of the village shop and postmistress of Mulconny.

Worzel stuck his head round the door.

"Oi! Is this here that there Ballydoon?" he asked.

Mrs. O'Rourke almost smiled at him in her relief.

"It is not, praise be to God. This is Mulconny. Ballydoon's another six miles."

"Is that a long way?" asked Worzel.

"Not as the crow flies," put in Mrs. O'Riley timidly.

"But I'm not a bloomin' crow," said Worzel. "I'm the bloomin' crow's worst enemy."

"Go straight through the village as fast as—I mean as far as

you can," said Mrs. O'Rourke hastily. "Then take the
footpath across the fields and you'll be in Ballydoon in no
time at all."

"Thank 'ee," said Worzel. The two ladies watched from
the shop doorway as he made his way down the road, cursing
at the rooks which swooped overhead. Mrs. O'Riley
shuddered.

"And Ballydoon's welcome to him!" she said, fervently.

Dusk fell, and on one side of an Irish hedge a tired Worzel
snored. In unison, on the other side of the hedge, Aunt Sally
snored too. And elsewhere in that same country, the
Crowman pedalled his bicycle in search of his errant
scarecrow.

Next morning, the labourer Rooney came upon Worzel,
who was just waking up.

"I'm thinking you've been sleeping rough," he remarked.

"I always sleep rough," agreed Worzel. "I try to sleep smooth, but as soon as I nod off I go all rumpled and crumpled."

"Ah, but there's many an empty cottage hereabouts," said Rooney. "Go through the woods there. You'll find a fine place to live in. If it's a big place you're after, it's smaller than that. But if it's a small place you want, you'll find it bigger."

This sort of talk was just what Worzel could understand. It was almost as daft as scarecrow talk, so it made perfect sense. He made his way in the direction indicated until he reached a small conservatory with a potting shed attached. His eyes lit up.

"Just wait till I finds my Aunt Sally!"

Aunt Sally was nearer than he thought. She had stumbled by chance on the same ideal dwelling, and was viewing it from the other side.

Inside, in the course of their investigations, they stumbled on each other.

"Aunt Sally!"

"Worzel!"

She moved as if to throw herself into his arms. Then, remembering her position, she fell elsewhere and tried to regain her dignity.

They were just beginning to argue about whose house it was, when the Crowman appeared on the scene.

"Well well well," mused the Crowman. "Worzel and Aunt Sally. I thought I recognised those dulcet tones."

Worzel jumped to attention.

"Mr. Crowman, sir! I just come this little titchy way to find

my Aunt Sally, sir. And now I'm going back."

"Oh no you don't, Worzel. We're staying here."

"Excuse me," said Aunt Sally. "But this happens to be *my* little big house."

"On the contrary, it happens to be mine," said the Crowman. He examined her label. "You are destined to live at the Museum of Folk History, Ballydoon Castle."

"Castle?" said Aunt Sally, in quite a different tone of voice. She turned to Worzel. "*I'm* going to live in a castle, where I belong. Where you're going to live, heaven knows. In a ditch, I shouldn't wonder."

She flounced out.

"I have changed my mind about going back," said the Crowman to Worzel. "I shall ply my trade over here. And as for you, Worzel . . ."

He led the way to the crossroads, and erected a scarecrow pole there. As Aunt Sally swept regally past on her way to the castle, a doleful Worzel was standing in position.

Round his neck was a placard. **Scarecrows made to order. Apply the Crowman, Mulconny**, it read.

Worzel began his first working day in Ireland with a sulk.

Rescuing Aunt Sally

Mrs. O'Rourke, Mulconny's postmistress and
shopkeeper, stood in her doorway one morning,
passing the time with her friend Mrs. O'Riley. A sudden
commotion made them turn, just in time to see their own
children racing past them.

"There's that Mickey of yours up to no good again, Mrs.
O'Riley," remarked Mrs. O'Rourke placidly.

"With that Mary of yours to help him, Mrs. O'Rourke,"
replied Mrs. O'Riley.

After the children came the strange figure of Worzel
Gummidge, riding a donkey.

"Come back here, you pesky humans—I'll teach 'ee to go
throwing stones at me and hitting me on the nose, so I will!"
roared Worzel.

Mrs. O'Rourke turned to Mrs. O'Riley.

"Wasn't that the Widow Mullins' donkey?"

"I doubt it," replied Mrs. O'Riley. "It doesn't take kindly to strangers."

The donkey chose that moment to toss Worzel off its back. That done, it brayed happily.

"On second thoughts, Mrs. O'Rourke, I believe it *was* the Widow Mullins' donkey," said Mrs. O'Riley.

Mary and Mickey returned to see if Worzel was hurt.

"Oo—there's a lump like an egg on my head," moaned Worzel, sitting up in a pile of hay. Mickey looked.

"That's not a lump like an egg. It *is* an egg," he remarked. "The Widow Mullins' hen must be laying again."

"Better not let her catch you," said Mary. "You can come and clean up in our house if you like. It's not ours really—we just pretend it is. Really, it's part of some disused stables."

Inside the dingy building Worzel brightened up considerably.

"My my my, this *is* a nice little house and no mistake," he said. "You can shove off—it'll do me nicely."

Mary's answer to that was to march on him with a pitchfork.

"I'm hungry," said Mickey. "Let's go and see if your mammy's giving any cakes away, Mary."

"Cakes?" cried Worzel. "Why should anyone in their right mind give away cakes instead of eating them?"

"They're just the stale ones she can't sell in the village shop," said Mickey. "She only gives them to Mary and me, though. Ordinary folk have to pay for them."

"Ordinary folk!" shouted the outraged Worzel. "I'm not ordinary folk! Just look what I can do with my head! Pass me that turnip there."

Mickey passed him a large turnip, and Worzel began frantically to pull and twist at his head, in an effort to get it off his shoulders.

While all this was going on Rooney had called on the Crowman.

"Ah, Rooney," said the Crowman. "You've come from the Widow Mullins?"

"I have not, sir," replied Rooney.

"Oh, really?" said the Crowman. "But I thought you were to collect the scarecrow I'm making for her."

"That's right, sir," agreed Rooney.

"Then you *have* come from the Widow Mullins?" repeated the bewildered Crowman.

"I have not, sir," said Rooney. "I've come from my own cottage where I've been eating a bite of dinner. But I have come for the scarecrow, and she would like to pay you in eggs and butter."

"Ah! Barter!" said the Crowman.

"That's right, sir—butter," said Rooney.

"I'm afraid the scarecrow isn't finished yet," said the Crowman.

"More's the pity," said Rooney. "I cannot wait. Do not fret yourself—I'll find the travelling scarecrow-maker. He's a tinker by trade but he'll always find the time to knock you up a cheap scarecrow."

Agitated by this sudden loss of trade, the Crowman ran after Rooney who was now on his way out.

"You shall have a real, live—I mean, proper scarecrow!" he cried. He led Rooney down to the crossroads. "Worzel Gummidge is his name!"

"'Tis a fine name," said Rooney, as they reached the crossroads. "A pity there is no scarecrow to go with it!"

Angrily the Crowman stared at the vacant scarecrow pole, wondering where Worzel could be.

Worzel was feeling angry too. Just as he had put on the old turnip instead of his head, to impress the children, they had run off and left him! Left him to grope blindly around the floor for his head all by himself . . . and now he had got his head back on at last and pursued them into the village, they were stuffing their faces with stale cake without thought of saving a crumb for him!

"It ain't every human gets to make friends with a scarecrow," he said, in an effort to get a slice of cake.

Mary held her cake out of his reach.

"It isn't every human that wants to," she replied.

"I could teach you a special language that nobody else can speak," said Worzel, and rattled off some Worzelese. Mickey and Mary shrugged, and began to speak to each other in Gaelic.

"He's a museum piece, really," said Mary. "I'm thinking, Mickey, that we could sell him to the Museum at Ballydoon."

Worzel forgot all about cakes and languages.

"That there museum is in that there Ballydoon where my Aunt Sally is. Oo ar! The Crowman told me. They've got her in a glass case, so they has."

"Who's Aunt Sally when she's at home?" asked Mary.

"She's my intended, bless her little wooden head," said Worzel soppily. "So how would you like to help me rescue her?"

"Is it a *real* Aunt Sally?" asked Mickey. "From a fairground coconut shy?"

"Oo ar!" said Worzel, nodding violently.

"Will you listen to that, Mary!" shouted Mickey, taking an interest for the first time. "We could start our own fairground with it!"

"Hey—that isn't the idea at all!" said Worzel. But the children had already set off in the direction of Ballydoon . . .

At the entrance to the museum a smart commissionaire eyed the trio with disgust.

"You children can't come in on your own. And *he's* not coming in because he's a vagabond. A ragamuffin. Be off with you."

"Right, we'll go," said Worzel. "All four of us."

"Four?" said the commissionaire. "Where's the other one?"

"In there," said Worzel, pointing past him into the museum. "We'll just go and fetch him."

"See that you do," said the commissionaire. "And be quick about it—hey! Just a minute!"

He realised his mistake too late, for by the time he ran after them, Worzel and the children had vanished down one of the museum's many corridors. A sob, often heard before, soon led Worzel to a large glass case, in which Aunt Sally stood, rigid but weeping. They tugged at the bolt holding the case door in place, but it would not move.

"Run for it, Mary!" cried Mickey, suddenly, for the commissionaire had found them. They scattered, leaving Worzel sticking by his beloved Aunt Sally, who by this time was seething with rage as he wrestled with the bolt.

"Don't 'ee get all hot and bothered," said Worzel soothingly. Just then, the bolt flew open and Aunt Sally stepped regally out. The commissionaire returned from unsuccessfully chasing the children, and barred their way.

Turning, they came face to face with the Crowman, who could always find Worzel when he needed him.

"Which is the way out?" demanded Aunt Sally.

"I don't rightly know," said Worzel. "That way's prison, and that way's the way to me being chucked on the bonfire."

Aunt Sally immediately chose the bonfire direction, and headed for the Crowman. But just then Mickey hissed: "Over here!" and both Worzel and Aunt Sally left by way of the window.

On the way back, in a borrowed handcart, they met Rooney

and a very badly-made scarecrow which was clearly the work of the travelling scarecrow-maker.

"That's a very fine scarecrow you have there," said Rooney, looking thoughtfully at Worzel. "I'll tell you what, Mary and Mickey. I'll give you my scarecrow for your scarecrow. And ten pence." The children shook their heads. "Twenty? My scarecrow and fifty pence, then."

Mary and Mickey nodded, and Worzel, had anyone been watching closely, could be seen to shudder.

The Crowman, riding through the village some time later, was pleased to see all the village children throwing balls at the captive Aunt Sally. Mary and Mickey were taking the money.

"That'll keep you out of mischief, Aunt Sally!" mused the Crowman, and moved on.

Something made him glance upwards at the Widow
Mullins' chimney, farther along the road. There, tied to it,
hung Worzel, his arms out in the scarecrow manner.

"And that'll keep *you* out of mischief too, my friend!" said
the Crowman approvingly.

King of the Scarecrows

In the solitude of an Irish field, the Crowman lifted high a simple twig as he prepared to perform the most awesome of scarecrow rituals—the giving of life to a new scarecrow.

This particular example of the Crowman's work was even uglier than Worzel Gummidge, but it was definitely completed. The Crowman solemnly broke the twig over its head.

"Apples for health, corn for plenty, berries for happiness,"

he began. "By the wind and the rain and all the seasons, I name this scarecrow . . ."

At the crucial moment in the mystical naming ceremony, a horse neighed. The Crowman paused and turned round, just in time to see a movement in the hedge. His eyes narrowed. He turned back to the scarecrow.

"On second thoughts, I'll name thee and give thee life when prying eyes aren't watching," he said quietly. He raised his hat courteously and moved away in the direction of his tricycle.

He had been right to think that someone was watching him. Hidden in the hedge was a tinker who pedalled the neighbourhood as a travelling scarecrow-maker.

As he rode off down the lane there was a mighty clap of thunder which almost persuaded him to go back and finish the job anyway. The elements could not be relied upon to keep out of such magical business as his own. However, within a few minutes all went quiet, and the Crowman decided it was safe to ride on.

Had he not been out of sight of the new scarecrow he would have been very worried indeed. For as the thunder roared the new scarecrow jerked, slumped, and jerked again, as if on the point of coming to life.

No one was watching Worzel Gummidge at that moment. He had decided that it was knocking-off time, and had left his post as rook-scarer in a neighbouring field. He was now craftily stealing a freshly-baked pie from a cottage window-sill, where it had been left to cool. Tucked under his arm was a bottle of milk, to which he had helped himself further up the village.

"My! If there's one thing nearly as good as a cup of tea and a slice of cake when the day's crow-scaring's done, it's a bottle of milk and a rhubarb pie," he remarked contentedly. He began to sing. "Ho, twelvety men went for to mow, went to mow a meadow . . ."

The Crowman, cycling along the same road, frowned in annoyance at Worzel's tones. He pedalled faster towards the voice. Round the corner, the song came to an abrupt halt as Worzel dived into the bushes for cover. The Crowman cycled on, and Worzel resumed his course with a huge sigh of relief.

"Cor, that was a near one and no mistake!" he gasped. "Best make thee-self scarce, Worzel, in case his searchitude comes back!"

He headed for a nearby field and looked delightedly at the sight that met his eyes. Company! Another scarecrow! He rushed up to it at once.

The scarecrow failed to respond.

"Oi!" yelled Worzel. "Don't you know your scarecrow greetin' yet?"

There was a pause.

"Oo ar!" said the scarecrow at last, lurching on its pole.

The travelling scarecrow-maker, about to drive away in his horse and cart, heard the babbling scarecrow talk from the other side of the hedge. Curious, he returned to his previous spying spot in time to see Worzel and the new scarecrow concluding the scarecrow greeting.

"I'm Worzel Gummidge—what's your name?" asked Worzel, when the formalities were over.

"I wasn't called nothin'," replied the scarecrow. Worzel could hardly believe his ears.

"He's turnin' them out so fast he's forgettin' to finish them off proper!" he exclaimed to himself. Turning to the scarecrow he said: "Until you've been given your name, you ain't been properly brought to life."

"Haven't I?" said the scarecrow. "Is that why I tumble over when I try to get off my scarecrow pole?"

"It must be," said Worzel. "Here—how about me giving you one? I know how it's done. Now, just let me find a twig."

He soon found one, and holding it over the scarecrow's head he began the chanting about apples for health and so on, just as the Crowman had done before.

"I name this scarecrow . . . now what *shall* I name this scarecrow?"

Suddenly the twig snapped in his fingers.

"Dangnation take it!" spluttered Worzel in exasperation. There was another loud clap of thunder.

"Now what have I done?" said Worzel in a worried sort of way, looking nervously around him. "Maybe I shouldn't name this scarecrow at all . . ."

He was jolted out of his mood by a large lump falling at his feet. It was the new scarecrow.

"Your Majesty!" it slobbered. "Now I have a name, I am properly alive!"

"I ain't given you no name!" shouted Worzel.

"But you have, Your Majesty," said the scarecrow. "Dangnation-Take-It!"

"You're even dafter than I am," said Worzel. "Dangnation-Take-It ain't no name!"

"It's a wonderful name and I thank you for it, O King of the Scarecrows," said the new scarecrow in an adoring voice.

Worzel began to think again. King of the Scarecrows? If Aunt Sally got to hear about this, marriage to him might hold fresh attractions.

"You can kiss my boots," he said. "Left one first. Then you can escort me to my palace . . ."

In the true palace of scarecrows, which might otherwise be described as the Crowman's workshop, the travelling scarecrow-maker was trying to butter up the Crowman.

"I've *seen* your powers, Master," he said in wheedling tones. "Scarecrows walking and talking—by daylight."

"You leave my scarecrows alone, do you hear!" shouted the Crowman. The visitor delved into the folds of his cape and produced a bag of money.

"Keep your gold!" roared the Crowman. "I've no scarecrows to sell *you!*"

The Crowman was unable to settle down to any more work after the tinker had gone so he set out for a walk to the village.

Here, another shock was awaiting him. He came face to face with a scarecrow—and one of his own making at that. One which, to his knowledge, he had not yet brought to life.

"Mildew Turnip!" he exclaimed, using the name he had chosen for this scarecrow. "What are you doing?"

The new scarecrow was in a hurry. King Worzel the First was proving to be a difficult monarch. He had already devoured eleven cups of tea and slices of cake, and he, Dangnation-Take-It, was having to find yet more. In a small place there is a limit to the amount of cups of tea and slices of cake available, and Dangnation-Take-It was having to improvise with a load of jam tarts from an unattended baker's van and a can of lemonade. And now here was a daft human calling him by a name totally unfamiliar.

"Get out of my way!" he snapped.

"Is that how you speak to me?" said the astonished Crowman. "Don't you know who I am?"

"Oo!" cried the scarecrow. "You must be Worzel's Aunt Sally! He told me to look out for her!"

"Do I look like Aunt Sally?" thundered the Crowman.

"How do I know, if I've never seen her?" asked the scarecrow. "And why did you call me Mildew Turnip?"

"Because Mildew Turnip happens to be your name, Mildew Turnip," retorted the Crowman.

"No it ain't," snapped the scarecrow. "It's Dangnation-Take-It. Given me by His Royal Majesty, King Worzel the First."

The Crowman's face darkened. He set off in search of Worzel . . .

"It was all a game, sir!" blustered Worzel, caught in the act of accepting homage from a fellow scarecrow, while wearing an eiderdown robe and a toffee-tin crown. "I didn't mean no harm."

"It makes no difference," said the stony-faced Crowman. "You know the penalty. There can be no appeal."

At midnight Worzel was hunched over the table in the Crowman's parlour, a pot of tea and a cake in front of him. Try as he would, he could not enjoy it, for he could see the Crowman outside stoking up the bonfire—and he knew it was for him.

"If I'd been a good scarecrow . . ." mused Worzel wistfully, as the Crowman came to fetch him.

They stepped outside and then the Crowman stopped for a moment to listen.

"Who's there—in the shadows?" he asked sharply.

The travelling scarecrow-maker moved forward into the light.

"It's only me, sir," he whined. "I was wondering, maybe . . . If you don't want this scarecrow any more . . . Perhaps I could have him?"

The Crowman looked at Worzel. "Well, do you want to go with him?"

"Is he like you, sir? Can he breathe scarecrows to life like you do, sir?" asked Worzel.

"After his fashion," said the Crowman. "Look!" As he spoke two poorly-made scarecrows jerked into view. They looked, to Worzel, like walking robots. "These scarecrows cannot talk or think—and they can move only at night," explained the Crowman.

"If I go with him, will I be like *them*?" asked Worzel.
The Crowman nodded.

"But you'll be saved from the bonfire, Master Gummidge,"
said the travelling scarecrow-maker enticingly.

"Only comin' alive at night, and not talkin' nor laughin' nor
singin' nor lovin' my Aunt Sally?" continued Worzel. "No
thank you very much. I'm ready, Mr. Crowman—for
whatever's in store."

"Begone!" said the Crowman sternly to the travelling
scarecrow-maker. He turned to Worzel. "Get back inside and
finish that cake while I put out the bonfire."

"Put out the bon . . . bonfire!" exclaimed Worzel in
amazement.

"Yes," smiled the Crowman. "You chose wisely, Worzel. You're not all bad after all. Now eat up your cake and off to bed with you!"

He went off to throw some water on the bonfire, and when he returned there were only a few crumbs to show that a cake had ever been upon the table. Smiling, the Crowman made ready for bed and went into his bedroom.

The smile on his face faded as he beheld Worzel, sitting up in the bed, eating the last of the cake.

"Not *my* bed! Get up at once!" he shouted.

Everything was back to normal.

Worzel's New Job

Worzel Gummidge, on his scarecrow pole, was having to put up with the most undignified treatment. Mickey and Mary were pulling the straw from his stomach.

"It can't be walking and talking one minute, and made out of straw the next," said Mary.

"What's this then?" asked Mickey, holding up a handful of Worzel's insides.

"Oi!" yelled the outraged Worzel. "You put that there

stuffin' back, afore I knocks the stuffin' out of you!''

Mickey obeyed.

''That's better!'' said Worzel. ''Course I's alive when I wants to be. Bet you'll be bumsnizzled if you ever saw anyone like me afore!''

''Bet you we have,'' said Mickey scornfully. Mary backed him up.

''Oceans of times!''

''We can show you one now if you don't believe us,'' added Mickey.

The disbelieving Worzel trudged after the children as they made their way across the field. The Crowman, passing by some minutes later, shook his head in exasperation to find that Worzel had gone missing again.

By then, Worzel was watching the labourer Rooney, as he marched up and down another field, scaring crows with the aid of a large drum.

"That ain't no scarecrow! Thass that daft human what don't talk no more sense nor I do!" snorted Worzel.

Mickey shrugged.

"He's scaring crows though—so he must be a scarecrow."

"And he's walking and talking too, isn't he?" added Mary. The pair of them then scampered off, leaving Worzel to grumble about their trickery.

"It ain't fair, so it ain't," muttered Worzel as he walked along the side of the hedge. Suddenly he tripped over something and fell flat on his face.

"You clumsy scarecrow!" came Aunt Sally's voice, its bitter tones ringing through the air.

Worzel, picking himself up, saw that she was tightly wedged inside a wheelbarrow.

"Don't just stand there, you ignorant hayseed!" went on Aunt Sally in scorching tones. "Help me up!"

Worzel obliged.

"Whoops-a-carrot-top, there we are!" he said, as Aunt Sally was hauled out. "What was you doin', Aunt Sal, wedged up all tight in that wheely thing?"

"Wedged up tight? I wasn't wedged up tight. I was watching the parade go past."

"Parade?" asked the puzzled Worzel.

"Why, that there military parade, that there military gentleman, you ignoramus—marching up and down that field with a drum," said Aunt Sally haughtily.

Just then the Widow Mullins appeared, coming to call Rooney to other tasks. Aunt Sally flounced off.

Worzel followed Rooney and watched where he left the drum. Maybe Aunt Sally would watch him as admiringly as she had watched Rooney, if he played it for her. But Rooney saw him making off with it and gave chase.

Desperate to get away, Worzel fell over the postman's motor-bike and sidecar which stood idling in front of the Widow Mullins' house. Horrified, he found the machine coming to life underneath him, and before he knew what was going on, he was careering down the lane, the postman's parcels and packets flying out behind him.

Aunt Sally, trudging down the same lane, heard the approaching motor-bike and turned to look over her shoulder. Seeing that it was Worzel, and with the idea of a lift in mind, she smiled sweetly at him.

Worzel, alas, could not stop. *Zoom!* went the motor-bike past Aunt Sally. And *splosh!* went the muddy water from the puddle nearby . . . all over Aunt Sally, so that she was drenched from head to foot.

What Aunt Sally said was anything but sweet. But Worzel was well out of earshot. Aunt Sally sat on the ground and sobbed.

Some time later Rooney stood in the Widow Mullins' living-room, gazing with the Widow Mullins at the bedraggled figure of Aunt Sally on the sofa.

"I'm going along, minding my own business, and there's this great dolly lying in the ditch," explained Rooney.

"What size of child would own a doll like that, Rooney?" said the Widow Mullins in amazement. "I'm thinking it must belong to the Castle Museum at Ballydoon. I'll wash and iron the poor soul's clothes, and then you'll take her back there. And now I have a little job for you, Rooney . . ."

The little job took Rooney to the Crowman's house, where he found the Crowman busily putting Worzel together again after he had crashed the motor-bike.

"Saints preserve us, sir," said Rooney, looking at Worzel. "That's an ugly feller if ever there was one! It's the Widow Mullins that's asked me to call round. Herself was wondering whether you were making the clothes-props at all?"

"My sole occupation is the ancient craft of making scarecrows," said the Crowman, somewhat offended at being asked for such lowly objects.

"Then you'll find it hard to make a living round here," replied Rooney. "A feller needs to turn his hand to several things. Good-day to you."

"Wait!" said the Crowman, looking at Worzel with a smile. "How long a clothes-prop would you be wanting?"

So it was that Worzel found himself holding up the Widow Mullins' washing line. It was some time later, when his arm was beginning to ache, that he noticed the exact nature of the washing he was propping up.

"Well, I'll be bumsnizzled! Them's my Aunt Sally's clothesies! Stand here all day I would, until Christmastime or Tuesday-Friday, to get them dry."

Inspired, he straightened up and propped the line up for a while longer. Then he began to think again.

"Hang on—if them's Aunt Sally's clothesies, where's Aunt Sally?" he wondered. "Aunt Sal! Where is you?"

Worzel dropped the washing line, and began to pace about in an agitated way.

"I'll take her clothesies to her, so I will," he decided, picking up the now muddy garments from the ground. He went off in search of Aunt Sally, calling her name.

"Shove off!" said Aunt Sally, from the Widow Mullins' front room. "I'm wearing my unmentionables."

Worzel, undeterred, looked in at the window. A large pot of geraniums knocked him back again. When he stood up he saw that Aunt Sally was wearing vest, bloomers and petticoat, all in pretty white broderie anglaise.

"I've got a sort of pressie for you—only they're yours already," said Worzel, holding out the clothes. Aunt Sally snatched them out of his hand.

"My dress! My beautiful dress! What's happened to it?"

"It's been washed that's what," said Worzel. "Only it fell in the pigswill."

"Fell in the pigswill!" echoed Aunt Sally in outrage. "I wish you would fall in the pigswill, you . . . you . . ." She was speechless with anger. She stalked of, leaving Worzel shaking his head forlornly.

He shuffled home looking crestfallen. The Crowman sighed as Worzel appeared.

"Can I trust you to do nothing?" he asked in exasperation. "How's the Widow Mullins' washing going to dry?"

"It weren't my fault," Worzel started to explain. "If Aunt Sally hadn't . . ."

"That Aunt Sally's nothing but a nuisance!" interrupted the Crowman. "Come on then. Back you go. You'd better be a scarecrow again. You don't seem to make a very good clothes-prop!"

With that the Crowman marched Worzel back to the crossroads.

"You'd better stay away from Aunt Sally," he warned Worzel, as he put him back on his pole. "She brings you nothing but trouble."

The Crowman walked towards the village, shaking his head. It was no good warning Worzel, he knew. He would always get himself into scrapes chasing after Aunt Sally. His thoughts were interrupted as he saw Rooney walking towards him, carrying the bedraggled figure of Aunt Sally.

"I wonder . . ." mused the Crowman. "How'd you like to sell Aunt Sally to me, Rooney?"

"To be sure. Delighted!" answered Rooney, glad to be saved the trip to Ballydoon *and* to make some money.

And so it was that the high-and-mighty Aunt Sally found herself alongside Worzel in a field, scaring crows!

"Ain't no use snivellin' and weepin', Aunt Sal," said Worzel encouragingly. "You got to shout an' holler now an' then—so they don't take advantage of you."

A large crow landed on Aunt Sally's arm, and she wailed all the more. Worzel smiled contentedly. Aunt Sally would be all right, when she got used to it. And joy knew no bounds at the thought of days spent with Aunt Sally beside him.

The Competition

"**H**ow soon will you be needing this new scarecrow?" asked the Crowman, as he stood outside the clubhouse of the Ballydoon Golf Club.

The Club Secretary waved his hand in the direction of the first green.

"Any time after tomorrow—that's the day of our annual competition. Once that's over we'll be reseeding the greens, and we need to stop the crows from scoffing the lot."

"I'll start on one this afternoon," said the Crowman. "I've got an old scarecrow with me now—but I don't really think—no, I'd better make you one."

His gaze rested regretfully on the inert form of Worzel, who was crammed into his trailer which, with his tricycle, was parked some distance away.

Worzel was not at all interested in what the Crowman was thinking. He was glaring at the elderly driver of a posh car which was parked right behind him.

Next to the driver sat Rooney.

"What the blazes is it, Rooney?" asked the very angry driver. "How dare it park in my space!"

Rooney went to investigate.

"'Tis a three-wheeled bicycle, your honour, Captain Forsythe, sir, with a two-wheeled pull-along thing-a-ma-jig.

And one of the Crowman's scarecrow fellers sitting up in it as bold as brass!''

"Is he a member?" barked the Captain.

"Can scarecrows join the Golf Club, then?" asked Rooney.

"The Crowman, idiot!" roared the Captain.

"I don't think so, Captain," said Rooney.

"Then shift it, man!" shouted the Captain. "Oh—I'll do it!"

He leapt from the car and shoved the tricycle as far as he could. It lurched off down a slope and ended up, Worzel and all, upside down at the foot of a large tree.

Worzel, after a few loud remarks to the Captain's retreating back, studied his surroundings.

"My, my! That's a garden and a half, that is!" he said admiringly. As no one was about, he got up and went off to look around.

The Crowman took some time to find his missing vehicle, and on discovering that Worzel had gone, decided that he could waste no more time looking for him.

"Suit yourself, Worzel Gummidge," he said aloud. "Walk home!"

Worzel was not very far away, but his attention was fixed on Captain Forsythe and his long-suffering partner, Father O'Malley, who had begun their game of golf. Hovering nearby was Rooney, there to caddie for the Captain.

Father O'Malley's ball went soaring over Worzel's head.

"Dang me, 'ee's tryin' to 'it them pesky rooks!" thought

Worzel, gazing skyward. " 'Ain't got no chance with a titchy ball like that!"

Just as the Captain was about to take his shot, Worzel shouted to him. The Captain mis-hit the ball, which dribbled a short way down the fairway.

"Clear off, you interfering fool!" yelled the Captain to Worzel. "Give me another ball, Rooney. That one didn't count."

This time, just as the Captain raised his club to take the shot, Worzel tried again.

"Potaters, Mister!"

They all looked at him.

"If you want to scare them old rooks, you want to try chuckin' potaters at them. You won't hit many—but they're better than those titchy balls. And jumping up and down like you're doing generally does scare them off!"

Having done his good deed, Worzel wandered off to a nearby hollow which was filled with sand. In it, much to Worzel's amazement, sat Aunt Sally.

"What you doin' here, Aunt Sally?" asked Worzel.

"I should've thought that was obvious, even to an uneducated apology for a horse's dinner such as you—making sandpies, of course," said Aunt Sally. "I'm on my holidays, you straw-stuffed barmpot!"

"But this ain't the see-saw," said Worzel, cautiously. "There ain't no sea."

"The tide's out, you brainless haybag!" shrieked Aunt Sally in exasperation. She made another sandpie. Suddenly a small white ball hit her on the back of the head.

"Pardon!" she said, unaware of what exactly had happened, but used to being knocked about by wooden balls at the fairground.

A second ball hit her on the head. It was too much for Worzel. He leapt to his feet.

"Dang me, Aunt Sal! They're chuckin' titchy balls at your head!"

He hurled them back.

Getting their balls back rather surprised the Captain and Father O'Malley. Gazing towards the bunker they became aware of Worzel's tousled head bobbing about in it.

"You unmitigated bounder, sir!" roared the Captain.

Worzel could not believe his bad luck.

"It's that crackpot human that was shoutin' and hollerin' at me!" he remarked. Aunt Sally stood up to see. One look at the Captain and her eyes misted over.

"Oh, Worzel! He's a sporting gentleman! My little heart is going pitter-pat! I must have a word with him."

She climbed out of the bunker and set off towards the Captain.

"Oh, sir!" Worzel heard her say. "Are you a kind gentleman who would save me from the unwanted attentions of that . . ."

Worzel saw the pointing finger and made off smartly.

"Check that he leaves, Rooney!" ordered the Captain. "If I were you, ma'am, I'd give up this loitering on private golf-greens."

"I will indeed, sir," said Aunt Sally sweetly. "But I was wondering if I might accompany you around the course, just to be on the safe side."

"You can caddy for me, if you like," said the Captain, dumping his heavy bag of golf clubs over her shoulder. Aunt Sally buckled under the weight, but bravely bore up, and the Captain and Father O'Malley proceeded to the next tee.

The following afternoon Mickey and Mary went to see Worzel. They had come to ask him if he would be going to watch the Golf Club Championship Competition.

"Don't you talk to me about no Golf Club," muttered Worzel. "My Aunt Sally was there yesterday, flitterin' an' a'flutterin' her eyes at that daft human with the 'airy face an' funny clothes."

"He means the Captain," said Mickey to Mary.

"The Captain wins the championship every year," said Mary.

"He wouldn't if I were playin'. If I had the right head for it, I would," said Worzel.

It was obvious that Mickey did not believe him.

"Come on," he said to Mary, and together they made for the door. Mary wanted it to be true. She called out:

"The Crowman's making a sporting scarecrow right now— I heard him telling me mammy. Perhaps you could borrow it."

When they had gone, Worzel set off for the Crowman's workshop . . .

Down at the Golf Club, the Captain was way ahead of the rest of the competitors, and approaching the last green. Behind him struggled the weary figure of Aunt Sally, bent double under the weight of the Captain's golf bag. The Captain could see no reason why he should pay Rooney to do it when Aunt Sally was willing to caddie for nothing.

"It's an awful shame, Father O'Malley," remarked the Club Secretary. "But there's no one to touch the man. He'll win again this year."

"Our day will come, Mr. Secretary," said Father O'Malley calmly. "One day the good Lord will set down a new champion among us."

At that very minute Worzel was creeping down one of the clubhouse's corridors. A new sporting head was clutched firmly under one arm.

"Reckon I'll find some togs in here, and plenty of titchy balls and sticks for hitting them with," he thought to himself. "Now I'll change my head . . ."

Just as the Club Secretary was forcing himself to award the trophy to the Captain amid reluctant applause, Worzel

emerged from the clubhouse. He looked so peculiar that all but Aunt Sally stared in disbelief. She immediately dropped the Captain's clubs and clasped her hands together in joy. "My hero!" she breathed.

Worzel strode towards the Captain, who was just accepting the cup from the Club Secretary.

"I'll challenge him!" he announced.

The Crowman, watching, recognised the head.

"A sporting head, all right, Worzel," he murmured to himself. "But why did you have to choose the wrong sport?"

The Captain accepted the challenge. He and Worzel approached the fairway.

Aunt Sally, no longer caddying for the Captain, handed a club to Worzel. He put the golf ball in position. He tossed the golf club to one side, and kicked the ball instead!

With a variety of spectacular leaps and dribbling skills, Worzel raced off down the fairway, displaying all kinds of ball control and dazzling footwork.

Aunt Sally's mouth dropped open in horror, as all around her the crowd began to laugh.

Finally, having kicked the ball into the hole on the first green, Worzel did a lap of honour.

"You stupid scarecrow!" screeched Aunt Sally, as the Captain returned to collect the silver trophy from the clubhouse.

Worzel began to blub. "Why didn't your magic work?" he asked the Crowman.

"My magic *always* works," said the Crowman. "The head you borrowed was never meant for the Golf Club. I haven't even begun work on it yet."

"Then what . . ." began Worzel.

"That head is intended for a new scarecrow for the Ballydoon Football Club," explained the Crowman.

Worzel looked mournfully at the angrily departing back of Aunt Sally.

"I've made a fool of myself in front of Aunt Sally."

"No, Worzel," said the Crowman. "You made a fool of yourself—as always—*because* of Aunt Sally."

Mickey

Mary

Mildew
Turnip

Aunt Sally

The Travelling Scarecrow-maker

Father O'Malley